APARTMENT 4A

Book 1

PJ Gray

SADDLEBACK
EDUCATIONAL PUBLISHING
www.sdlback.com

APARTMENT 4A: BOOK 1
OUT OF CONTROL: BOOK 2
DEAD HELP: BOOK 3

SADDLEBACK
EDUCATIONAL PUBLISHING
www.sdlback.com

ISBN-13: 978-1-62250-708-5
ISBN-10: 1-62250-708-8
eBook: 978-1-61247-959-0

Printed in the U.S.A.

20 19 18 17 16   2 3 4 5 6

AUTHOR ACKNOWLEDGEMENTS

I wish to thank Carol Senderowitz
for her friendship and belief in my abilities.
Additional thanks and gratitude to my family and
friends for their love and support; likewise to the
staff at Saddleback Educational Publishing for
their generosity, graciousness, and enthusiasm.
Most importantly, my heartfelt thanks to
Scott Drawe for his love and support.

APARTMENT 4A

Bree stood at the window of apartment 4B. She was looking down at the dirty alley. She wondered where her older brother, Andre, was.

Sometimes her brother would be gone for weeks. Sometimes he would come back drunk. Sometimes he would come back just to sleep. Her brother did not like to talk.

Apartment 4B was in the back of the building at the end of the hall. Bree shared it with her aunt and brother. They had lived there a long time. Since Bree was a little kid.

Bree and Andre moved into apartment 4B with their aunt after their mom died. "Your mom died from drinking too much," their aunt always said.

Bree was almost three years old when her mom died. She did not remember her.

Bree's aunt was old and sick. She was too sick to work. Her aunt sat in the apartment all day. She watched TV until she fell asleep.

"Call the landlord," her aunt would yell. "Those people next door woke me up again!" She would say this every day before Bree went to work.

"I never hear anything next door," Bree would tell her. "You don't know what you're talking about."

Bree never saw anybody next door at apartment 4A. It was the only other door at the end of the hall. Bree never saw anyone coming or going. She saw very few people in their building. Nobody else lived on their floor. Most of the other people moved out long ago. They moved when the landlord raised the rent again.

ON THE JOB

Bree left high school last year. She did not finish. She had to make money to pay the bills. She got fired from a fast food job. She did not come to work because her boyfriend punched her in the face. She did not want to come to work with a black eye. The manager was her boyfriend's friend. He fired her. Bree lost her job and left her boyfriend on the same day. She did not trust men.

Bree found a new job at a messenger company. The company delivered letters and packages for money. The boss paid Bree with cash for each delivery. Bree wanted to find a second job to make more money.

Mona worked at the front desk. She took phone orders. She was Bree's only friend. And the one person at work who was nice to Bree. She liked to talk to Bree when Bree was in the office.

"Does your aunt still hear people next door?" Mona asked.

"Yes, I think she's losing her mind," Bree answered.

"Can you call the landlord?"

"No, he lives out of town. We don't want any trouble." Bree did not want to tell Mona their rent was behind.

Bree saw a picture of Mona's kids on her desk. Mona liked to talk about them. "Mona's a good mother," Bree said to herself. This made Bree think about her own mother.

Bree never saw a picture of her mother.
Her aunt burned all the pictures years ago.
Bree never knew her mother's real name.
Her aunt only called her Tutu. That was her
nickname. Her aunt always got upset when
Bree asked about her mother. So Bree
stopped asking.

NO ONE THERE

Bree came home from another day at work. She got to the front door of her apartment. She could hear the TV. She did not want to go inside and deal with her aunt.

Bree looked at the door of apartment 4A and wondered. She opened the hall window and stepped onto the old fire escape. She was afraid when she looked down. Bree did not like heights. She got dizzy and started to shake.

Bree carefully looked into the window of apartment 4A. She saw nothing. No furniture. No people. It was empty. She tried to open the window. It was stuck.

Bree came back into the hall to her front door. Why did her aunt hear voices from apartment 4A? Bree wondered if her aunt stopped taking her pills. She could not walk well. And she did not want to see the doctor.

"Is that you, Andre?" Bree's aunt called out from her chair. "Get out of my house!"

"No, it's me. It's Bree."

Bree's aunt looked at Bree through her thick glasses. "Andre was here looking for you," her aunt said. "He wants my check. He knows I always give it to you."

"When did he leave?"

"Just now," her aunt replied. "Watch out for him. He's been drinking, and he's mad."

Bree had not seen Andre for a week or so. He spent more time on the street. Bree knew he drank. She did not know if he was doing drugs. "He can't get our money," Bree said to herself. Bree loved her brother but had to protect herself.

Bree left the apartment to buy some food for dinner. She had no money to buy a new lock for the door.

HER FIRST MEETING

Later that night, Bree was in bed. Her bed was the living room sofa. Bree could not sleep. She could hear her aunt snoring from the bedroom.

Bree wondered if Andre would come. Would he be drunk? Would he try to get her money? Bree hid her money inside one of her shoes in the closet.

Just then, Bree heard a sound from across the hall. It was coming from apartment 4A.

Bree walked slowly to her front door. She put her ear on it. Bree heard the sound of a woman. The woman was crying. She slowly opened her front door to look into the hall. Bree saw the door to apartment 4A. It was slightly open.

Bree quietly walked to the front door of apartment 4A. She slowly pushed it open. The apartment was silent. Bree saw a woman on the living room floor. She had long black hair and wore a dirty blue dress. The woman was not moving. Was she asleep or dead?

Bree looked around the room for other people. "Hey," Bree said softly. "Are you okay?"

The woman did not move. Bree bent down to feel the woman's arm. It was ice cold.

Bree ran out of the room and into the hall. Should she tell her aunt? Should she call the police?

She stopped to think. Her mind was racing. Her heart was beating fast. Bree turned around and walked back into apartment 4A. She wanted to see if the woman was alive.

The woman was gone.

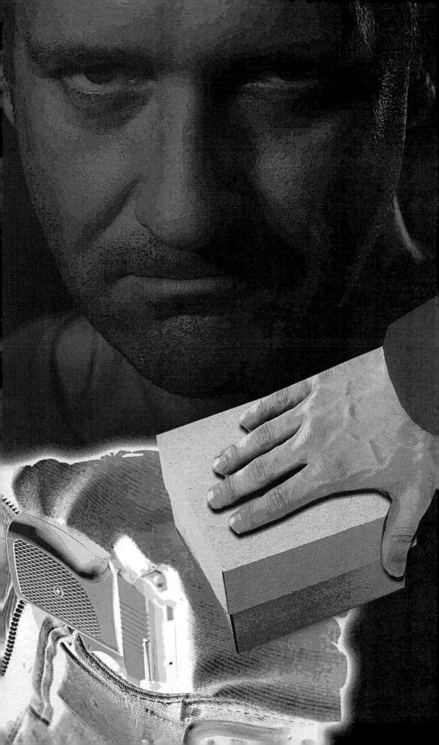

BAD NEWS

Bree went to work the next day. She wondered about the woman in apartment 4A. Bree sat in the front office with Mona and waited for some work.

"Was that woman dead in apartment 4A?" Bree asked herself. Was she a dream?

"Bree!" Mona called out. "Bree, the boss man wants to see you."

Mr. Edwin was her boss. He did not talk much and never smiled. Bree stepped into his office. She closed the door. Mr. Edwin wore a brown coat. She saw a gun under it.

"Take this box to two ninety-nine Baker Street," Mr. Edwin said. "Do you know where that is?"

"Yes," Bree replied.

"When you get there, put the box in the trash can. It's next to the gate."

"Okay," Bree said.

"Don't let anybody see you," Mr. Edwin said.

Bree took the bus to Baker Street. She walked to 299 Baker Street. She did not like this place. Nobody lived in this part of town. The street was filled with old, run-down buildings.

Bree saw the trash can. She looked around. All clear. Bree put the box in the trash can and ran. She got to the bus stop. She took the first one home.

Bree did not want to go back to Baker Street. She did not want to work for Mr. Edwin. She knew he was bad news.

She came home and opened her front door. Andre was there. He pushed past her to leave. "Where have you been?" Bree asked.

"None of your business," Andre replied. "Did you cash her check?"

"No," Bree said. "Her check hasn't come."

Andre moved closer to Bree. He put a knife to her face. "You liar," Andre said. "I don't want to hurt you. But I will."

Bree took a deep breath. She could smell him. He smelled like booze. Then Andre turned and walked down the hall. He went down the stairs.

Bree's aunt was crying in the living room. "Get out of my house!" her aunt cried out.

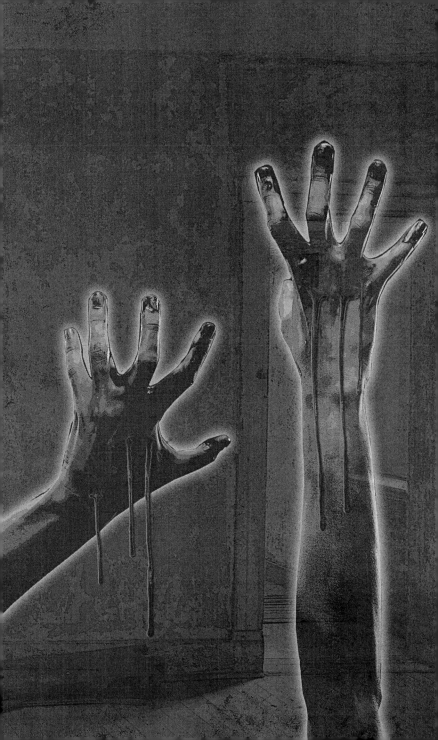

THE WOMAN RETURNS

Bree could not sleep that night. She kept thinking about her brother. Andre was in trouble. He never used to care about money. He could not keep a job. He only wanted money to drink. But now he needed it. Was it drugs?

At that moment, Bree heard a cry from the hall. It was the woman in apartment 4A. Bree jumped from the sofa. She ran to the door. Apartment 4A's door was open.

Bree ran into the apartment. She saw the woman standing in the living room. Bree saw tears on her face. The woman looked at Bree. She said, "Go get help!"

"Who are you?" Bree asked. "Why are you here?"

"Go get help before it's too late."

Then the woman lifted her arms to Bree. Bree saw blood on the woman's arms. It dripped onto the floor.

Bree screamed and ran out the door. She ran back to her apartment to get a towel for the blood.

Bree ran back into apartment 4A. But the woman was gone. The room was silent. Bree stood alone in the room. There was no blood on the floor.

"What the hell is going on?" Bree asked herself.

JUST LIKE TUTU

Bree came home from the food store. Her aunt was sitting in her chair in front of the TV. Bree asked her aunt about the sounds from next door.

"I need to ask you about the sounds you hear," Bree said.

"Yeah. There's screaming. Crying all the time," her aunt replied.

"Do you hear a woman cry?"

"Yes," her aunt said. "Now hush. I'm trying to watch my show."

Bree wanted to know more. She took the food out of the bags. "Do you hear other people? Or just the woman?" Bree asked.

"Shut up, girl!" her aunt yelled. "You make my head hurt. You're just like your mama."

"How am I like my mother?"

"Tutu drove me crazy just like you. Tutu was bad news. She stuck me with you and Andre."

"Why do you call my mother that?" Bree asked.

"Shut up! Leave me alone," her aunt replied.

Bree could tell her aunt was sick. She slept more than normal. She ate less than normal. She did not want to see a doctor.

ANOTHER JOB, ANOTHER BOX

Bree went back to work. She did not want to go. But she needed the job. She needed the money.

Mona was not at work that day. She called in sick. Mr. Edwin sat in his office. He asked Bree to step in.

"I need you to take this box to a new place," Mr. Edwin said. He handed Bree the small box. It was heavy.

"Take it to three forty-nine Pine Street," he said. "Do you know where that is?"

"Yes," Bree replied.

"Put the box in the trash can at the side of the building," Mr. Edwin said.

"Okay," Bree replied.

"And don't let anyone see you."

Bree took the bus to 349 Pine Street. She sat on the bus looking at the box. "What's in this box?" she asked herself. She shook the box, but it made no sound. She wanted to open it. It was sealed with heavy tape.

Bree got off the bus and walked to 349 Pine Street. Nobody lived on this street. All the homes were empty. The windows were boarded up.

Bree saw the trash can and put the box inside. She walked away and hid behind a tree. She wanted to see what would happen.

Bree saw a man walking down the street.
It was her brother. He did not see Bree. He
was looking around. "Is he looking for me?"
Bree asked herself.

Bree ran behind another building and down
an alley. Andre never saw her.

She took the bus home.

THE KISS

It was late at night. Bree could not sleep. She waited for Andre. She had not seen him for a week. Did he see her put the box in the trash can?

She heard a cry from apartment 4A. It was the woman. Bree was really scared. And she felt very cold.

Bree got up slowly and walked across the hall. The front door of apartment 4A was open. Bree saw the woman standing in the living room. She saw no blood this time.

"My baby keeps crying," the woman said. "He won't stop." The woman looked out the living room window. The moonlight was bright.

"Who are you?" Bree asked. "I can help you. Let me find help."

"No, don't go," the woman replied. "Come closer to me."

Bree was scared. She walked to the woman. Bree wanted to see if she was real.

The woman reached out and felt Bree's face. "You're sad," the woman said. "And you're mad at the world."

Bree could feel the woman's hand on her face. It was cold. The woman moved slowly. She kissed Bree's cheek. Bree closed her eyes.

Suddenly, Bree felt very warm. Her body felt warm. She felt happy. Bree had never felt like this. "Is this love?" she asked herself.

The woman smiled at Bree. Bree felt a cold wind in the room, but the windows were closed. Bree could not talk. She closed her eyes.

Then the woman looked away. "He keeps crying," she said. "Make him stop crying! I can't take it anymore!" The woman ran to the bathroom.

"Wait! Stop!" Bree called out.

Bree tried to stop the woman, but she was too fast. The woman ran into the bathroom and slammed the door. Bree tried to catch her but could not.

Bree opened the bathroom door.

The woman was gone.

THE TRUTH
ABOUT TUTU

It was the next night. Bree sat on the sofa. She could not sleep. She could hear her aunt snoring in the bedroom.

Bree could not stop thinking about the woman. Who was she? Why was she there? Why did her arms bleed? Was she real?

Bree heard crying. It was the woman in apartment 4A. She ran across the hall to the empty apartment. Bree opened the door. She saw the woman in the living room.

"Who are you?" Bree asked the woman. "Tell me your name."

"My poor Andre," the woman said. "My poor baby's in danger."

"Andre?" Bree asked. "My brother?"

"He needs help! You must help him!"

"Wait," Bree said. "What's your name? Tell me your name!"

"They call me Tutu."

The woman looked at the living room window. It was closed. "My baby!" she cried out. "Help him!" She ran to the window.

"No!" Bree yelled. "Please stop!"

The woman ran across the living room. She jumped at the closed window. She put her arms up to cover her face. Bree could hear the sound of breaking glass. "No!" Bree screamed as she saw the woman jump.

Bree ran to the window. The glass was unbroken. She looked at the street below.

The woman was gone.

ABOUT THE AUTHOR

PJ Gray is a versatile, award-winning freelance writer experienced in short stories, essays, and feature writing. He is a former managing editor for *Pride* magazine, a ghost writer, blogger, researcher, food writer, and cookbook author. He currently resides in Chicago, Illinois. For more information about PJ Gray, go to www.pjgray.com.